❀ ❀ ❀

ALSO BY REEM FARUQI

Unsettled

Lailah's Lunchbox

Amira's Picture Day

I Can Help

Golden Girl

REEM FARUQI

HARPER

An Imprint of HarperCollins*Publishers*

Library of Congress Control Number: 2021951263
ISBN 978-0-06-304475-3

Typography by Carla Weise
22 23 24 25 26   PC/LSCH   10 9 8 7 6 5 4 3 2 1
❖
First Edition

TO ZHHTRO: ABBA, AMMA, HAMZAH, TALHA, AND OSMAN

AND FOR ALL THOSE WHO ARE WAITING TO BE REUNITED

WITH THEIR LOVED ONES . . .

BEFORE

THE

INCIDENT

PART ONE

LIPS

I DIDN'T DO IT.

I promise.

These are the words Abba said
right before they took him.
But if you were to zoom in
on me like a camera lens
and focus on me,
just me,
I'd say
Yes.
I did do it.

If you were to look at me,
eyes level, lips sealed,
and ask me,
just me,
about all the incidents,
I would have said something different.

I DID DO IT.

The first time
was an accident.
The next few times,
not so much.

THE FIRST TIME

Loud Blaring Music
Zaina, shimmying to "Sheek Shak Shok,"
shimmied so hard,
she knocked her desk
and her pineapple-scented
pink lip gloss glided
right into the laughing mouth
of my bag.

MY NAME

Aafiyah

AH-Fee-YAH.

When we pray,

we ask for khair—

goodness—

and aafiyah—

well-being—

to be protected from problems.

When you're healthy,

have money,

are happy,

you have aafiyah.

Everything good.

Just like me.

MY BEDROOM MIRROR

I tried it on.
Shimmery
Shiny
Glide-y
Lips.

Zaina's lip gloss looked better on me.

Guilt
smells
a little
like pineapples.

BEST FRIEND

Zaina
got tall,
grew in other places too,
sighs at you

when you ask where she's from
(half Pakistani, half Lebanese).

But when it's someone she wants to talk to
(usually a boy),
she makes her mouth
soft.
She makes her eyes
smile, says
Wanna guess?

MY BODY

I want
to GROW
in all the right places,
but my prayers haven't been answered . . .
yet.

MY FAMILY

Abba
is my father.
My grandmother:
Dadi.
My grandfather:
Dada Abu.
My brother:
Ibrahim.
Mom was supposed to be
Ammijan,
but when I
said *Mommy*
finger-painted her name in pre-K
she smiled
let the word stay
let it warm her
like golden sunlight on skin.

AAFIYAH QAMAR

Teachers quack my name
into Quamar.
Teachers ask:
No *u* after the *Q*?
No.
Pronounce the *Q*
like a *K*.
But actually,
if you really want to get it right,
the *Q* is an Arabic qāf, ق.
Feel the sound in your throat
when you say my name.

UPTIME

When I have
downtime,
Mom makes me watch Ibrahim,
which sounds easy but is really
hard.

In the tub,
I make the water bubbly for him
shampoo spikes through his curls
tickle anywhere to make him laugh,
then finally hand him off to Mom
for a nap.
Free at last!

I get Abba
to take me to the courts
(only him because he's the best player),
so that downtime
feels more like
uptime.

I stretch my legs
arms and shoulders
twirl my racket while I wait for Abba's serve—
   very fast.
I hit the tennis ball back
         even faster.

After we've practiced for an hour,
Abba lobs balls
up
up
up
in the air.
I have my eyes
on them.
One at a time
the balls come
D
O
W
N

My feet shuffle magic
lift my left hand high
the moment when contact is made.

Balls land right on the line.
Gold popping everywhere.

IN-BETWEEN TIME

After tennis,
my lips turn up
when Zaina texts
 A to Z?
Which means
Come over.

My name begins with *A*, and
Zaina = *Z*,
so we have
A to Z meetings,
which is just us hanging out
at her house.

The good thing about
where I live
is that Zaina is only
three lookalike houses
away from me.

Hanging out means
lounging on the couch
scrolling through
our favorite pictures
until Zaina's mom,
Naheed Aunty, yells
Get Off Your Phones!

Then hanging out means
lining up rounded pawns,
spiky castles,
and our favorite:
the queen.
Chess.

But today Zaina
doesn't reach for the chessboard.
Let's go upstairs . . . , she says.

ZAINA'S ROOM

Look what Salma gave me!
She wasn't using it.

The benefit to having three older sisters:
all their stuff.

The benefit to having a two-year-old brother:
not much.

Zaina opens a purple case,
a shiny mirror
followed by
shimmery circles of eye shadow
that close together
with a snap.
The sound of hope.

Zaina puts the eye shadow palette
in her drawer
where old phone chargers
and gum wrappers
kiss.

SECOND GRADE

When I was in second grade,
we read about Johnny Appleseed,
learned he had "itchy feet,"
which meant he loved to travel.

I must have "itchy fingers,"
because I love to borrow.

HOMEWORK

When Zaina runs down
to get her binder
from the kitchen table,
I have 30 seconds
on my own.

30 seconds
is enough.

I break up the kissing cords
and gum wrappers
slide my hand around
put the palette
in the hollow cavity
of my book bag.

PROBLEM

I like the feeling
of something new in my hands.
I like the feeling
of something new in my hands
                    that's not mine.

BATHROOM MIRROR AT HOME

This eye shadow
makes me look
creepy.

THE NEXT DAY

Zaina's eyebrows s t r e t c h
Did you see my palette?
Guilt nibbles my insides
when I shake my head no.

SCHOOL LIBRARY

Girls in my class
check out
chapter books
(fiction which is fake)
about fluffy cats and dogs.

But the boys and I
love
Weird but True! books.

I check out as many as I can,
read for hours,
copy my favorite facts
into my notebook
that has a flap and a lock
that says: *Keep Out.*

You never know when you'll need the perfect fact . . .

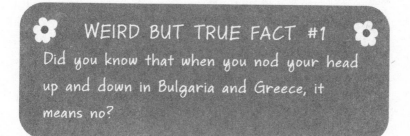

WEIRD BUT TRUE FACT #1
Did you know that when you nod your head up and down in Bulgaria and Greece, it means no?

Maybe in another country
shaking my head no to Zaina
means yes?

ZAINA'S MESS

My sisters give me things
only to take them right back . . .

Muzna told me
my room is so messy
I probably lost the eye shadow here.
Zaina makes her eyes
roll
her shoulders
lift
her breath
exhale.

Zaina whirls
I don't think my room is so bad,
is it?
as she trips on her laundry.
We laugh.

WHAT I DON'T SAY

I think I like your room too much.

WHAT I DO SAY

_____

Too busy giggling.
Zaina's laughter
always tickles me
in the right places.
Wherever Zaina goes
there's laughter.

I giggle when something's funny,
but Zaina laughs long and deep.
Her laugh is like floating stairs
each note lighter than before.
Her laugh makes something funny

even funnier.
Her laugh makes you   p a u s e
and join right in.

THINGS I RETURNED

Eye shadow
    it didn't look good on me.

OPPORTUNITY

When Naheed Aunty calls
her
to put the milk back in the fridge,
I put the eye shadow back
where I found it.

Told you . . .
I just *borrow* things.

THE LIP GLOSS

Still borrowing it
            for now.
(It looks better on me.)

BEST FRIEND

The good thing
about having a best friend
is when they know what you like to eat
and don't have to waste time asking.

The bad thing about having a best friend
is knowing where everything is in her house.

ZAINA'S ROOM

Zaina has a disco-ball lamp
and when the sunlight
dances on the ball
it sprinkles little squares
on her cream ceilings and peach walls.

Zaina has a dresser
full of tangly necklaces, makeup cases, and shirts
   with stripes.
But the drawer at the bottom
is the candy drawer.

Zaina hides Twizzlers, Airheads, gummy bears
in lip gloss–bright colors
and anything that is sweet, gummy, and chewy.

I like chocolate
not candy
so Zaina makes sure to collect chocolate too
     just for me.

Zaina loves the feeling
of sweet in her mouth.
She orders pineapple on her pizza
but when I'm over
she orders it on half
and green peppers
and onions
for me.

I like that she doesn't even need to ask.

THE SISTER I NEVER HAD

Zaina has three big sisters
and a grandmother
who likes to gift them matching clothes.
But as the big sisters grew,
they protested.
They didn't want to match.

But Zaina and I
loved to match
so her grandmother would send clothes
for her "little friend."
Me.

Zaina and I
would make sure
our mothers would do our hair the same.
One day
a fat side braid
or
two equal ponies
or
six skinny braids.

And we would wear the same number of bangles
on each arm
and pretend to be sisters,
or even better, twins.

When aunties would pretend
to not know who was who,
it made me feel special
warm inside
like we were really sisters.

So now when
we're at the masjid,
even if we don't match
(now we don't really do it)
and one of us isn't there,
aunties will say . . .
Where's your twin?

SELF-PORTRAIT

I wasn't always pretty.
My nose too big
like a samosa.
My cheeks too round
like gulab jamuns.
But then
I turned 13
and the aunties stopped squeezing my cheeks.
My face grew
to match my nose.
My cheekbones
sucked up the baby fat
and even though
people still call me cute,
they're wrong.
With Zaina's lip gloss on,
I'm gorgeous.

DISBELIEF

Sometimes
when I look in the mirror,
I can't believe
     It's

          Me.

          Actually me.

That's when the trouble started.
People were so busy
looking at my face,
my curled eyelashes
(it's Vaseline),
they forgot to look at my hands.

CONFESSION

No one knows my secret.
No one.

But now you do.

GOLDEN HOUR

I love taking photos
with the new Canon camera
Abba gave me.

Abba teaches me
to hold the camera steady
to be a light seeker.

(There are so many different kinds of light.)
Gray, white, dull, bright
and my favorite
when the light is like butter
so good you want to hold it until it melts

at golden hour
before the sunset
or after sunrise
my kind of hour.

Abba teaches me to make the shutter speed
High
Very high
when capturing Ibrahim.

It's the only way I can freeze him
stop him in motion.
Amazing how I can look through such a
tiny
viewfinder,
the world so small,
but once the click click sounds,
the camera smiles and sighs.
I see the picture
on the back of a screen
the world enormous again.

FIA Q

Ramona Quimby
called herself Ramona Q.
I'm Aafiyah Qamar
and sometimes: Fia Q.

Zaina calls me Fia.
Mom and Abba FooFoo.
Dadi and Dada Abu say my name
with a strong 'ayn, ع,
at the back of their throats.
Aafiyah.

Ibrahim says Fiyaaa like a question.
Says Aaf, then waits for me to say Fiya,
laughs like it's the most hysterical thing
    in the world . . .

MY BROTHER ON GOOD DAYS

When Ibrahim smiles,
his eyes shine.

I love how I can
see his smile
when I'm behind him
because his cheeks puff out.

I love how I can
tell before he laughs.
When I hold him,
his belly shakes
and shimmies with joy.

MY BROTHER ON BAD DAYS

Ibrahim is naughty,
always climbing things
chairs
dishwasher
coffee table.

Always putting small things in his mouth
    Abba's cuff link
    Mom's earring
    my Legos
    my old doll's blueberry pie.

Mom shakes her head
tells me
I wasn't *this bad*
but
what would she say if
she knew
the real me?

🌸 WEIRD BUT TRUE FACT #2 🌸
Did you know that one theory states that
the moon is a broken piece of Earth?

QAMAR

In Arabic my last name
Qamar
means the moon.

Sometimes when I borrow things
and guilt swirls in my mind,
I feel like a

b   r   k   n
b   o   e

piece
of my family.

PART TWO

EARS

For me,
that fact is false.

HEARING LOSS

I would ask Mom
What?
all the time
when she would talk softly.
Until one day
she said
I think we need to get your hearing checked . . .

At the ear nose throat clinic,
patients are older than Dada Abu.
I don't want a hearing aid!

Mom gives me a look
with no words needed
that makes me shush.

TV

Can we put on the
closed captions,
please?

I'M REALLY FINE

Before I step
into the scary booth,
there is a sign that says:
"Signs You Have Hearing Loss."

That's irony
A sign that says *signs* . . .
Get it?

SIGNS OF HEARING LOSS

I seem to have a few of them.

TRUTH

Fine.
I seem to have many of them.

THE DOCTOR'S WORDS

No need
for a hearing aid.
You have mild hearing loss
in your
      right ear.
We'll keep an eye on it.

You may not be able to hear
certain frequencies as well.

MY WORDS TO MOM

I probably have mild hearing loss
because I'm always watching Ibrahim
and he's always screaming in my ear.
You know that, Mom?

But Mom acts like she can't hear me
as we drive away . . .

IRONY

The doctor said
to keep an eye on my hearing loss.
Shouldn't he have said ear?

NIGHTTIME TEST

When I lie on my right side
I hear the crickets
crystal clear.

But when I lie on my left side
Silence.

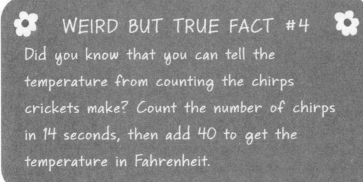

🌸 WEIRD BUT TRUE FACT #4 🌸
Did you know that you can tell the
temperature from counting the chirps
crickets make? Count the number of chirps
in 14 seconds, then add 40 to get the
temperature in Fahrenheit.

Telling the temperature
without a thermometer
is pretty cool
if you ask me.

At school
I usually sit near the front
next to Zaina.
At home
I like to use closed captions on the TV.

I don't like when people
talk to me
when it's dark outside
and I can't see their faces.
I don't like that my mouth keeps asking
What?

PART THREE

❀

GUT

WAITING

Even though my face changed
I'm still waiting for my body to catch up.
Zaina isn't.

Her body grew
not just tall tall tall
(now I have to focus the camera lens up at Zaina)
but her shape changed
so I have to zoom my lens out w   i d   e r.

When the light's just right
Zaina is always ready.

When Zaina looks at the camera
she changes her face
tilts her head
squints her eyes
pouts her lips
arches her back
puts one hand on her hip
then the other.

I want to tell Zaina I like taking candid photos
but Zaina leans in
like she's going to tell me a secret
fiddles with the long necklace
on her long neck.

Sometimes people think I'm 15 or 16!
Zaina wipes her sweaty cheeks.
Bronzer streaks the backs of her hands.
It must be the makeup . . .

I'm 28 days older than Zaina,
but people think I'm 12.
I wish I looked
older.
More sophisticated too.
Sometimes when I'm with Zaina
I feel left behind . . .

OUR FATHERS

Zaina's father fixes hearts
(a heart doctor).
My father fixes airplanes
(an airplane doctor).

I wasn't always pretty
but
I was always well-off.

Abba works in aviation.
His company chops planes up
into pieces,
sells airplane parts,
has offices all over the world.
An airplane's insides
and outsides matter.

I wish my insides were better.

SUNDAY SCHOOL

I wish I knew
how to
stop
borrowing things.

I wish microbes in my gut
could tell me
when to stop.

READ

Sometimes when I read books,
Abba says,
The cool thing about knowledge
is that no one can steal it from you . . .

I wish I could tell Abba
about my problem.

IRONY

We learn about it in school.

For example,
    a pilot who is afraid of heights,
    a fire station that burns down,

a girl who has money
but borrows things?

PART FOUR

FINGERS

LUNCHTIME

Ms. Sullivan
has a rainbow prism
made of glass.
She keeps it on her desk;
it reminds me of Zaina's disco-ball lamp.
It catches the sunlight
and shines it around the classroom
in different shapes.

At lunch
I forget my water bottle,
go back to get it.
See the rainbow catcher,
feel my heart go
thump thump thump.
That feeling in my stomach
punch punch punch.
The itch in my fingers
tingle tingle tingle.

I grab the rainbow catcher
just to see what it feels like.
The weight feels right
a little like joy.

I put it back
but I pick it up
to feel joy again
and before I know
what I'm doing
(I was going to put it right back)
I zip it up in my bag.

No one knows.

LUNCH

My stomach feels like
a washing machine,
going round and round
round and round.

The joy I had
is gone
lathered with dread.

Even though Mom packed
my favorite lunch,
aloo gosht with rice,
I barely take a bite.

THE SUN

At home,
I stuff the sunlight catcher
under my mattress,
into the darkness
where Ibrahim can't get it.
When Mom puts him down for a nap,
I take it out,
puff out the breath I didn't know I was holding,
smile as I watch
the sun's new shapes
on my bedroom walls.

THE NEXT DAY

Ms. Sullivan emails our parents
tells them her prism is missing:
it was given to her years ago
by her mom.

She already spoke to the class.
Could they speak to their children,
just to make sure?

DINNER

Do you know where it went?
It's an easy shrug,
even though my shoulders feel rubber-band tight.
My head shakes no,
even though it feels like someone's knocking.

We could always buy her a new one?
I mumble.

I don't feel hungry anymore
even though Mom made aloo gosht with rice again,
my favorite.

THE NEXT DAY

At lunch
before I go to the bathroom,
I peek into her classroom.
No one is watching—
I put the prism right back.

No one knows.

WHY I DO WHAT I DO

In fourth grade
social studies
we learned about
needs and *wants*.
Needs like food or shelter.
Wants like lip gloss or a rainbow prism.

It's not like I *need*
the things I take
and I know I could buy

58

the things I *want*.
But when I see the things I *want*
right in front of me,
I *need* them.

I know
what you're thinking—
Aafiyah Qamar, just STOP.

Believe me,
I've tried.

But I can only stop
when the thing I want
　　　—Need—
is safe in my hands
or even better . . .
my bag.

GOD

God knows of course.
But if you were to look at
a   l   l
the things I've done,
I really am good.

It's just this one thing I do.

I borrow things,
sort of like a library book.
I usually bring them back
except sometimes
I don't.

PART FIVE

HAIR

SUNDAY MORNINGS

Are for video calling
Dadi and Dada Abu.

Dada Abu has cancer,
but you can't tell through the screen.
His hair still puffy,
his smile still wide.
(It gets wider when we tell him
we can only see his forehead
and he moves the phone down.)

2 weeks left
until winter break,
until we meet again . . .

2 WEEKS LEFT

Until we go to Pakistan.
This trip is happy—
we'll see our grandparents.
This trip is sad too—
Dada Abu and Dadi will come back with us.
Dada Abu must get the best treatment for his cancer—
I really hope Emory Hospital is the best . . .

SUNDAY AFTERNOONS

When Abba works on weekends,
and I want to make downtime
feel more like uptime

I ask

 Can we play tennis?

 64

Mom opens her mouth—
Go dust the living room
then you can think
of going someplace . . .

Again: *Please can we play now?*

But Abba's eyes glaze into
a t-w-i-n-k-l-e.
He puts his papers down.

Afoo, what's the Nike slogan?

Just Do It.

A fake sigh from Mom.
A wink from the clouds.
Abba grabs his racket.
Let's go.

ON THE COURTS

Nothing sweeter
than the sound of
the hissing
of a new tennis ball can
being opened.

On the courts,
nothing sweeter
than the sound of
your opponent's feet running
two steps behind
your ball
landing neatly
on the line.

THWACK!

COMPETITION

At tennis tryouts
Abba says: *Notice the competition.*
We haven't touched a ball yet,
so I judge faces
and bodies.

PONYTAIL

I smooth mine down.
Abba says I should be ready to play.
Who plays with their hair down?

INTRODUCTIONS

Coach Baker makes us go around
the circle,
say our names.
I say my name slowly and clearly.
A girl in blue's name is Ciara,
another boy's name is Connor
and a familiar face: Imran.

TENNIS COMPETITION

The girl in blue
(Ciara)
plays better.

Slices the ball harder.
Serves quicker.
Stronger backhand.

For now . . .

TRYOUTS

When Mom comes to pick me up
from tryouts,
Ciara whispers
Your mom's pretty

     But she isn't even dressed up . . .

READ

When I first learned
to read
in kindergarten,
I didn't stop at sounding out letters,
gluing words together.

I didn't just read words.
I learned to read faces,
eyes, and mouths,
to scan the thickness of eyelashes,
the color of lips.

When Mom is relaxed,
she wears no makeup.
When Mom is stressed,
she paints her face
outlines her eyes
colors her lips.

Today Mom's face is
just right,
blank as canvas.

MOM'S SHOES

When Mom picks me up from tryouts,
everyone notices her hot-pink heels
that click and snap their way over to me.
Not many of the other moms
wear shoes
like my mom.

I don't even know how to wear . . .
Mom says *flats* like

it's the plainest word in the world.
I'm so used to heels.
It's a habit . . .

I wonder if my borrowing
is a habit?

CONNOR

Hey Fiona—
I hate that I turn in response.
It's Aafiyah, I say.
Will you have to wear that
when you're older?

Connor circles his face.
He means Mom's hijab.

Because you're too pretty for it . . .

I don't know what to say.

WEIRD BUT TRUE FACT #6
Did you know that cuttlefish hold their
breath to avoid predators?

REASON WHY I DON'T HAVE A COMEBACK LINE

If all the other boys are moths,

then Connor is a butterfly.

RANKING

If I had to rank people by looks:

    1. Connor

    Definitely a butterfly.

    2. Imran

    the boy from the masjid

    Definitely a moth.

If I had to rank people by skills:

    1. Imran

    Probably a butterfly.

    2. Connor

    Something in-between.

In looks and skills:

Ciara: Butterfly

In looks and skills:

    Me: a butterfly in looks

    almost-a-butterfly in skills

THE NEXT DAY

If God made you pretty,
then why do you need to
cover up?

Connor takes his racket,
slides it on my covered leg.

If you just dressed
a little more like
Ciara over there . . .

Imran opens his mouth
then closes it.
Imran's mouth opens again.
He turns to Connor.
Hey, why don't you . . .

My voice comes back real quick.
I don't need anyone to speak for me . . .

WHAT CIARA WEARS

Very short shorts,
a tank top,
topped by a
waterfall of hair
splashing down.

I KNOW THE DRILL

Even though I'm
mostly covered,
boys stare.
Men look
for a second too long.

Aunties admire
but their eyes
don't smile.
Girls get jealous
and keep me
far away.

All except Zaina,
who knew me from long ago
when I was anything but
pretty.

COMPARISON

The thing is
even though people may look at me
for an extra minute,
people listen to Zaina
for lots of minutes.

Zaina's voice you can hear from upstairs.
Zaina's voice you can hear from downstairs.

Zaina's words have very little space between them.
She speaks loud and fast
and teachers are always telling her to slow down,
but I never do.

ON THE WAY HOME

Hey Mom,
if God made you pretty
then why do you need to
cover it up?

> God tests us
> with
> beauty
> wealth
> health.

> How you use your gifts
> is what matters.

> Do you use them for good?
> Or abuse them?

> Whether you're pretty
> or not,
> God wants you to wear hijab.

> The choice is yours . . .

TWO MOMS

Sometimes it feels like I have two moms.
One mom
doesn't wear makeup,
wears glasses
and sweatpants.

The other mom
wears contact lenses,
outlined eyes,
colored lipstick,
clothes with
buttons
zippers
frills
folds.

But they're the same person.

Sometimes
when Mom's dressed up,
my mouth gets shy.

MIXED DOUBLES

Coach Baker
pays attention to
how we play.
How we slice balls
down the line
crosscourt,
but not how our personalities mix.
He pairs Connor and me.

No fair . . .
whispers Ciara to me.

When we do drills,
I'm in the front
volleying balls.
But I notice
Connor
keeps hitting balls
in the net.

Net
Upon

Net
Upon
Net.

And each time
I'm bending
bending
bending
to pick up the balls.
I shoot Connor a look.

He smiles
so hard
his eyes make happy crescents.

I like the way you bend . . .

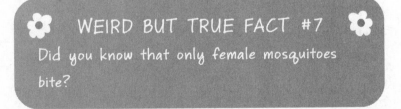

WEIRD BUT TRUE FACT #7
Did you know that only female mosquitoes
bite?

MY RESPONSE

I take a ball,
slice it at him.
I guess he wasn't ready.
Because this time
he's bending over.
The ball hits him in
the wrong area;
a giggle bubbles in my throat
to see him squirm.
If Zaina was here,
she would do *the laugh*.
But then Coach Baker
gives me a look
and makes me sit out
on the line.
Now.
No questions asked.

TENNIS PRACTICE

On the sidelines
tennis isn't so fun anymore.

When Mom picks me up,
she's wearing rosy lipstick
which means she's stressed.

Probably not the best day
to get in trouble . . .

PART SIX

TONGUE

PAKISTAN TRIP

Mom's stressed,
because Abba's stressed
about traveling to Dubai.

The rest of us are going to
Pakistan
and I can't wait.

My blue passport
matches my blue jeans.

Abba needs to travel
to shut down an office,
to fire some people
for something he won't talk to us about.
He sighs
like an old person
when he talks about work,
while Ibrahim and I
run in ovals around the conveyor belts.
Even though Abba sighs about work,

his aviation job has benefits,
one of them being
we get to travel first class.

When we get to the counter
of the business class lounge,
Abba looks happier already.
Who wouldn't?
Inside they have white sandwiches
without crusts
cut in perfect triangles.
And lounge chairs
that you sink deep into
where you can prop your feet up.
And a dark room
just for movies
with buttery popcorn
popping near by.

My feet feel all floaty,
my smile extra toothy.
Outside the shiny glass doors
I see a little girl staring at us
from a crowded waiting area

looking bored.
I put my thumbs on my cheeks
waggle my fingers
stick out my tongue
smile when she giggles.

Traveling to Pakistan
makes me feel like
a kernel of popcorn
waiting to pop.

PLACES I'VE BEEN

Germany

Austria

England

Kuwait

Qatar

Maldives

Hawaii

Pakistan

Bahrain

Turkey

FIRST CLASS

Your seat lies
all the way down
like a bed.

At night
when they turn the lights out
in our cabin
t-w-i-n-k-l-y blue stars
glow down at us.

You can sip hot chocolate.
Flight attendants hover by,
get you everything you need.
You can even ask
what color lipstick they wear:
Mac's Russian Red.

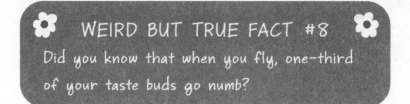

But I swear
the hot chocolate on board
is the best I've ever had.

WHAT I LOVE ABOUT PAKISTAN

I love going
to Pakistan
because that's where
Dadi and Dada Abu
live.

If you think we are well-off in America,
you should see us in Pakistan.

I love that I don't have to do any chores,
no loading my dish in the dishwasher
(there is no dishwasher).

Instead when I'm done eating,
a maid picks up my dish and washes it!
There are cooks, maids, washerwomen,
to wash my dishes,
serve me breakfast, lunch, and dinner
(tea as well),
wash my clothes
and iron them.

I love midnight Baloch ice cream
where your tongue is left buttery.
Hot N Spicy kabab rolls
where your tongue sweats,
craves water, mango juice, soda,
anything,
and the sound of my new shoes
tuk tuk tuk
on the polished mall floors.

TEATIME

Wheeled out on a golden trolley,
served on a white flowery lace doily
on a silver rectangular tray.

Warm cups
of milky chai,
steam tickling my face.
Round biscuits
in a square paper box.
String that once tied the box
now ripped off by Ibrahim.

Chocolate circles,
jelly circles,
salty circles too.

Perfect puffy triangles,
Golden-brown samosas.

We should do this in Atlanta every day.

WHAT I DON'T LIKE ABOUT PAKISTAN

The staring.

(Even if I'm fully covered
head to toe
with only my face peeking out,
they stare at you
as if you're wearing nothing.)

When I was little,
it was winks
from men on the street.
Now it's staring.

MUSLIM RULES

Muslims are supposed to
lower their gaze,
but I think
the boys and men

see me

    and forget?

WHAT I ALSO DON'T LIKE ABOUT PAKISTAN

The rich are rich
but
the poor are so, so poor.

I can't help feeling
sad and sorry
for the servants.

On the streets
girls my age,
boys too,
dress so differently.
Faces smudged,
begging for money.

BAZAAR

In the bazaar
rickshaws sputter.
Horns *PARP!*
Dadi makes me knot my tongue,
so the shopkeepers
don't hear my accent.
My broken Urdu,
my too-Americanness.
She doesn't want the shopkeepers
to make us pay more.

In the malls
Dadi lets me talk,
because the prices are fixed.

VILLA GARDEN

On the veranda
we sip cool mango juice
and nibble on pizza circles
that fit in your palm.

Dadi tells me I've grown
and to stay out of the sun
to stay fair.

But I can't,
don't want to stay out of the sun,
because I play tennis.

When I'm in the sun,
my skin gets dark,
but when Zaina's in the sun
(Zaina plays lacrosse),
her skin drinks it up,
gets golden bronze.

WHEN I KNEW I WAS GROWING UP

From Dolmen Mall,
I spot *the outfit*
in the window
t-w-i-n-k-l-i-n-g at me
under the lights.

Dadi points to it and asks the salesman to wrap it.
Barely glances at the price tag,
swipes her glowy credit card
and buys it for me in minutes.

The shalwar kameez
is the reddest red
I've ever seen.

Fits me like skin.
Look-at-me red.

When I put it on,
walk to the kitchen
past the cook and the helper boy

to get a glass of mineral water,

Mom whispers

I don't think you should wear that around here.

Maybe I am becoming like Zaina, too.

KARACHI

City of lights

Clothes the colors of butterflies

A breeze

that lifts me up

Morning

Noon

Night

Even the birds sound delicious.

FULL MOON

We've waited for
the night
with a full moon.

My entire family squeezes into the car—
cousins, khalas, mamus, Dadi, Dada Abu.
Shoulder to shoulder,
hip to hip.
There's no space to breathe
but plenty of space for laughter.

BEACH

At Sandspit Beach
the waves
greet us like
hugs.

At Sandspit Beach
we tiptoe
to holes of sand,
to peek at big sea turtles
digging digging digging.

The turtles
and their babies
will find their way to the sea,
find their way home.

And even though I live in Atlanta, Georgia,
born there too,
Karachi, Pakistan, keeps bringing me
back.

THE

INCIDENT

PART SEVEN

SHOULDERS

HEADING HOME

Back together
we meet Abba in Dubai.

Our skin is browner,
our smiles happier.
Abba's skin more tired,
his smile smaller.

When our boarding passes are scanned,
Dada Abu, Dadi, Mom, Ibrahim, me, Abba
beep beep beep beep beep BUZZ!
The lady behind the counter
scans Abba's boarding pass again,
but it doesn't go beep,
it goes
BUZZ!

Behind the counter
the lady asks Abba
for more ID,
reaches for her walkie-talkie.

Is there a problem?

WALKIE-TALKIE

For Ibrahim and me:
a game.
For Abba:
the opposite.

CHANGE OF PLANS

The lady behind the counter
asks question
upon question,
so we don't notice
the two men without smiles
until they surround us
and put a hand on Abba's shoulder.

Sir

> *Your name*
There is a criminal case against you
We need you to follow us

> > *Now.*

WHEN MATH IS WRONG

But

    I

        Have

          a

            Flight

              to

                Catch

These 7 words Abba says.

You have the wrong person.
5 words.

Whatever it is . . .
3 words.

I didn't do it.
4 words.

Add up to zero.
Nothing.

 108

CHANGE OF PLANS

The flight
will be rescheduled
and instead of reclining on
the seats that lie all the way back,
we sit and wait
on a very hard bench
in a police station.
This isn't first class.

STATEMENT

In language arts
we learned about statements:
sentences that don't ask a question,
or give a command,
or have an exclamation mark.

But here a statement
is something you give
that you don't want to say,
because your mind is buzzing
buzzing
buzzing
with questions
and exclamations.

???!!!

ABBA

Abba takes too many deep breaths.
I don't want him to get sick.

ABBA'S STATEMENT

Not guilty.

Ibrahim is asleep on Mom's shoulder.
I wish I could sleep like that too.
Normally I don't envy Ibrahim,
but now I do.

EMBEZZLE

Sounds like sizzle
or dazzle.
But when I ask Mom,
she says embezzle
in an ugly voice.
It means to take something that isn't yours,
to **steal**.

When Mom
says that word,
my toes
and fingers
feel shivery.

ISSUES

I thought having money was important
but
apparently having a passport
is more important.

A passport
means
passing through a port—an airport.

Abba's passport being taken away
by the police
is more like a
stayport.

BURJ KHALIFA

2 days ago
we were
in front of the tallest building in the world
taking a photo.
It was so humid
our sunglasses fogged.
We squinted into the sun
shoulder to shoulder
Abba, Dadi, Mom, me,
Dada Abu holding Ibrahim,
some smiles open
some smiles closed.

If you were to take the photo,
tear it at the three-quarters mark
where Dadi and Abba are,
that would be
our family now.

POLICE STATION WAITING ROOM

I hear my parents' voices
> *normalcy*
> *schedules*
> *passport*
> *chemotherapy treatment*

over and over.

Abba's words—
> *The rule here:*
> *Someone needs to give their passport*
> *as bail*
> *for me not to go to jail.*

> *I'll stay on Dadi's passport.*
> *You go back with Dada—*
> *Get him the treatment he needs.*
> *I'll be out of here soon enough.*
> *I'll get a good lawyer . . .*
> *All a big misunderstanding.*

Mom's words—

> *What happens if Dadi doesn't stay back,*
> *doesn't give her passport?*

Abba's words louder—

> *Then I go to jail*
> *even though I didn't do anything!*
> *Someone needs to give their passport*
> *on my behalf.*
> *Dadi has agreed.*
> *I want you to go home.*
> *Take the kids.*
> *Take Dada Abu for chemo.*

Abba smiles with his beard
but not with his eyebrows.

> *We are blessed*
> *to have family . . .*

My words, if they let me speak—

> *If we're so blessed,*
> *why are we here,*
> *in this mess?*

QUESTIONS

Do we have to leave Abba and Dadi?
> *Dada Abu needs his treatment.*
> *We live by the best cancer center*
> *in Atlanta.*
> *Abba and Dadi are coming back soon,*
> *very soon . . .*
> *inshallah*
> *Let's go.*

AIRPORT

Back at the airport
without Abba and Dadi.
We are leaving with
4 people.
We should be leaving with
6.

In the corner of my eye
in the corner of the waiting area,
I see a father,
mother,
and a little girl in the middle.
Their arms
hold the little girl's hands

                              h

                        g

                  i

            h

and when they lift their arms
the little girl floats in the air,
shoulders fly,
and even though she floats for just 2 seconds
she giggles way too long.

THINGS I HATE

Happy Families

ANOTHER THING I HATE

Flying economy class.
The seat doesn't lie all the way down
like a bed
and even when you try to put your chair down
it's still sitting up
which for a flight that's as long as
16 hours and 20 minutes
is not good enough.

The flight attendants don't smile the same smile at you
because they're too busy
trying to help too many passengers
who are squished too close together
and you don't get hot chocolate.

WITHOUT

ABBA

PART EIGHT

SKIN

WAYS I MISS ABBA

I miss Abba
when I change the toilet paper.
When the soft white squares
ran out
we'd holler
PASS THE TOILET PAPER!
Abba on the top stair,
me the bottom.

I'd throw the toilet paper up in a perfect arc
and even though our sport is
tennis, not football,
Abba caught the toilet paper neatly
yelled *TOUCHDOOOOOWN!*
spiked the toilet paper
on the ground
       with the most perfect
THUNK!
       you've ever heard.

TIME FOR SCHOOL

When Mom wakes me up for school,
she nudges me hard
and pulls off my blanket.
If I'm still not up,
she splashes water on my sleeping skin.

When Abba was here,
he would sit
with me in the mornings
on the corner of my bed
and talk talk talk to me
about life and the world
until I woke up for school.
When Abba was here,
he would say:
Wake up!
There's a monkey outside!

EVIDENCE

Abba requests his files of numbers
that add up to his innocence.
But the judge barely peeks at Abba's files
or Abba's face—
he just says *Guilty*
and minuses his freedom away . . .

COMPARISON

While I'm in school
eating spicy chicken
rolled in paratha,
I don't know
that Abba's wrists
are pinned together
in handcuffs,
that Abba is pacing
in a jail cell,
waiting
waiting
to get out.

DINNER-TABLE DISCUSSION

After 24 hours
Abba is let out,
a new court case set,
but his passport is still gone,
meaning he can't go anywhere
can't leave the country
can't come back
even if he wanted to.

The scary part:
Abba is trying again
for the judge to say
Innocent,
but if the judge says
Guilty
Abba goes to jail
for good.

ABBA SITUATION

Mom frowns,

pushes food around her plate.

Her voice gets angry

when she says

Abba's still stuck.

He's innocent

yet it's a game of waiting

while the case gets appealed.

Abba can't work

or get paid

or leave.

The person Abba fired

for embezzling money

(we have records to prove it)

got angry

and blamed Abba right back.

MOM HISSES

You'll see,
people who lie
people who steal,
if they don't get caught now
they'll get caught later.
Mom points upward—
And if not in this life
then definitely in the next.

GUILT

Makes my feet feel
really heavy.

Abba's accused of the thing
that I don't want to do
anymore.
Ever again.

THESE HANDS

Hug my baby brother

shampoo bubbles into his curly hair.

Bring juice to Dada Abu,

help Mom,

log into Skype with Abba and Dadi.

But these hands have borrowed too many things.

These hands are guilty.

These hands are going to do better,

I promise.

US EMBASSY

We write them
email after email.
Our father is falsely accused.
His American passport has been taken.
We are looking for assistance.

Please help.

We try emailing a senator.
Senator Johnson is away from his desk.

PASSPORT

Even though Abba's passport is
American Blue,
it seems like it doesn't matter
because his skin is
Pakistani Brown.

The lines in Dada Abu's face
get **bolder**
wearier
heavier.

PHONE CALLS TO US EMBASSY

We call
and call
and get the same answer—
Unless the criminal case is dismissed
there's nothing we can do to help . . .

PARTNERLESS

Zaina plays lacrosse,
doesn't like tennis much.
I should try harder to make tennis-playing friends,
but when you have one good friend,
you sort of forget how to make new ones.

With Abba gone,
I head to the courts alone.
I throw the ball high and serve
ball after ball
until I use them all up
(9 balls to be exact).

If Abba was here
and my serve zoomed past him,
it would be a perfect ace.
But no one hits them back,
just a regular boring serve.

TRANSPORTATION

When Abba was here,
I'd catch a ride
in his BMW
(the one we flew to Germany
on his fortieth birthday
to design and customize—
I helped choose the color).
Glacier green.

The BMW smells like
leather and hope.

Through traffic,
Abba makes the BMW glide,
dodging potholes and pedestrians, speeding
when the eye of the traffic light
turns
yellow,
almost red!

Even though we're in Atlanta traffic,
cruising and conversation
come easy.

NOW

Mom makes me
take the big yellow bus.
The bus that should be
the color of snot,
because that's all kids talk about.

The bus stinks.

The kids on the bus
talk about bodily functions
way too much.

You'd never call this ride
cruising.

AT SCHOOL

Without Abba,
I feel empty.
I want to feel better.

Zaina
has a brand-new
battery-operated sharpener
(it fits perfectly in my palm).
It's see-through
and blue and red.
When you push the pencil,
it whirs,
the sound of a circle
making pencils gleam.
When Zaina's mom picks her up early,
she leaves the pencil sharpener
on the rectangle of her desk.

I make my eyes
look out the window,
but it's not good enough.

The sharpener
teases me,
invites me to come closer.
I know that if I touch it
I will feel better.

Even though I try to
look away
my heart's beating,
stomach punching,
fingers tingling.

Before I know what I'm doing
(*or do I know what I'm doing perfectly well?*),
I look over my shoulder,
knock her desk just so
her sharpener tips over
and falls into the hungry mouth of my book bag.
Mine.

HEARTBEAT

Nice and s l o w again.

 138

AT HOME

I close my bedroom door.
Let the sharpener suck every pencil I have—
gray lead,
colored,
guilt sounds like whirring.
My pencils have never been
so sharp before.

EVENING

When the dark-blue sky
hugs the sun
and the sun goes down,
my mood goes down too.

These hands feel guilty
again.

THE NEXT MORNING

Zaina
looks looks looks
under her books,
in her pencil case,
in her book bag,
taps me on the shoulder.
Have you seen my sharpener?

My tongue tastes like guilt—
bitter.

I shake my head no.
She walks over to Ms. Sullivan.
I take her sharpener out
of my pocket
and slip it back where it should be.

DADA ABU'S CANCER PATIENT INSTRUCTIONS:

Avoid sick people.

Stay away from crowded places.

Don't eat fruit with its peel on because of bacteria.

Make sure to wash and peel your fruit carefully.

Get lots of rest.

Take your medicine the same time each day.

AFTER DADA ABU'S CHEMO

It doesn't take many days

for Ibrahim to get sick.

Just one.

IBRAHIM'S FEARS

Dada Abu wears a face mask
so he won't catch Ibrahim's germs,
because his immunity is low.
But Ibrahim doesn't like the mask.
It reminds him of monsters.
He wants Dada Abu to TAKE IT OFF,
which means a lot of crying and screaming,
and even though I have mild hearing loss
my ears hurt.

SICK BROTHER

You would think
that someone who is sick
would want to rest
or take a nap.
But instead
Ibrahim fights his nap,
gets freed from his crib.
Runs over to me while I
multiply and divide fractions,
traces my eyebrows
calls them *eyebrowns*.
Swings on the oven door
back and forth.
Runs back to me,
digs through my book bag,
rifles through my lunch money,
walks around with money in his mouth.
A closed smile,
laughing eyes,
until Mom grabs him.
Picks him
       up

Stop Putting Things in Your Mouth!

Scoops out the dime,

a penny too,

and tries to put him to sleep

again.

DADA ABU'S CHEMOTHERAPY TREATMENTS

Dada Abu

has his own pretty bowl.

Golden

sunflower petals

bending all around

and a plate

that looks like smashed

sunflower petals.

Dada Abu

doesn't want to eat out of

all the other bowls

or plates,
because each time he eats,
his bowl has to be disinfected
because of the strong medicines
he is forced to take.

But he has no appetite,
doesn't even want to eat from his bowl.

DADA ABU'S SUGGESTION EVERY DAY

I'll just eat on a paper plate.

*No need for you to go
through all this trouble.*

Mom's response—
Nonsense.

ABC JUICE

Every day
when Ibrahim watches
nursery rhymes on TV,
Mom makes Dada Abu's
ABC juice.

Because of pesticides—
She peels an apple
Extra
Peels a beetroot
Extra
Peels a carrot
Extra
Shoves the peeled pieces
into a juicer.

Makes a rosy drink
tinted with orange
froth that invites me
to take a sip.

Tastes like mud
Dada Abu says.

But how can something
that looks so pretty
taste so bad?

One day
when the juice is on a tray
and I'm delivering it to his room,
I take a teeny-tiny sip.
He's wrong—
It tastes worse than mud.

CHEMO

Once this chemo is over
I'm taking this bowl,
smashing it to bits.

The way Dada Abu
whispers it
so that Mom can't hear
makes us both laugh,
heaving-shoulder laughter.

UNFAIR

It's hard to hear
what Mom says
on the phone to Abba.
Even though I face
my good left ear
to the phone,
Mom turns her back to me,
speaks low on purpose.

But it's easy to read
her yellow notebook pad
next to her cold cup of chai.

It looks like
Abba's lawyer charges $100
+ $100
+ $100
+ $100
+ $100
+ $100
+ $100
+ $100
+ $100
+$50
= $950 an hour.

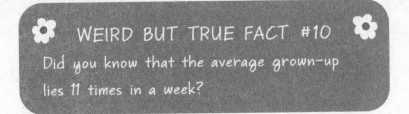

WEIRD BUT TRUE FACT #10
Did you know that the average grown-up
lies 11 times in a week?

Mom, are we running out of money?

No, Afoo. Why would you think that?

My mom just told lie #1.

JOB APPLICATIONS

Mom sits with her computer,
wrinkle not moving
between her eyebrows.
Scrolls through
page after page
but doesn't submit
an application.
Not one.

DECISION

So you know how much I love baking?

I make my eyes big
look down at Mom's sugar cookie in my hand
pretend that I had no idea.

Mom's hands move
when she talks,
which is all the time.
I applied to the bakery
but they have no spots.
Mom's hands stop moving.

MOM'S WORRIES

On a bright-yellow notepad
Mom usually tucks away
underneath her laptop,
but this time it's out.

At the top,
LIVE SIMPLER.
Find a smaller house—
different school district?
Sell gold from bank.
<u>No more shopping</u>
(this is underlined three times).
Find a job (this is in the biggest writing).
Follow up with US Embassy.
Get a better lawyer (more money???)
to get him back!

And then lots of numbers
that don't really add up . . .

 152

FACTS

We need money
to pay a better lawyer
to get Abba back.

CHEMO UNIFORM

Dada Abu hangs his jacket on his chair
folds his scarf
tucks in his gloves
button to button
loosens his shirt's collar.

> *Dada Abu, you can wear*
> *sweats . . .*
> *you know . . .*
> *comfy clothes to chemo.*

I prefer it this way.

INFUSION ROOM 4

On a plush chair
Dada Abu reclines,
but comfort is far away
from this room.

Cancer sucks, Dada Abu.

Dada Abu looks at me,
eyes more gray than brown,
smiles.
There's a hadith . . .

> *"Don't curse the fever.*
> *It removes the sins of a believer*
> *in the same way*
> *as a fire*
> *removes*
> *rust from iron . . ."*

So you see
I'm trying not to complain . . .

Even though the see-through liquid
drips from the IV,
soon to run out,
our conversation flows.

Nurse Donna comes by.
Dada Abu shares,
My granddaughter
knows weird and true facts.
Aafiyah, tell us one.

My eyebrows stand
while I think,
fingers skim the pages
of my notebook.

Dada Abu, did you know
you're a librocubicularist?
A librocubicularist is someone
who reads in bed.

And I like how Nurse Donna
doesn't say anything about how I look.
Instead she says,
What an intelligent person you are!

WRONG KIND OF GOLD

Nurse Donna comes back
looking like an astronaut.
I'm just suited up,
it's protocol
before I administer the chemo.

She has a big syringe
full of gold medicine . . .
The wrong type of gold.

CHEMO TIME

Nurse Donna wipes Dada Abu's skin,
sets a timer
for five minutes,
pushes her gloved finger
little by little
on the needle.

I watch Dada Abu's veins
drink the medicine,
sip it up
really slow.

I feel sick.

CAMERA LENS

Suddenly it feels like
my eyes
are looking through a camera lens,
like everyone's outlined
in black Sharpie.
Black dots
popping up
here
      there
            everywhere . . .

NURSE DONNA'S VOICE

An order—
Put your head between your knees,
I'll get you some juice.

Dada Abu
and I drink
orange juice
in Styrofoam cups.

Wooziness gone.

Hey Dada Abu,
don't tell Mom about today . . .

Dada Abu nods,
reassures me.
It happens all the time . . .

SIDE ROOM

Dada Abu
stands very straight.
Wait here.
Walks to the skinny room
on the side of the waiting area.
How much do I owe?
I haven't gotten charged yet . . .

Oh honey, don't worry.
You'll get your bills.

Do you know when?
No. But they'll come.
They always do.

MOM'S NEW JOB

So you know how
I'm pretty good at
organizing and cleaning?
My eyes roll.

My mother's face often
matches the kitchen floors
. . . flawless.

With Abba gone,
I wanted to help out.
I got a job!

    Congrats, Mom!

I clean homes now . . .
    You're a maid?

I'm a death cleaning specialist,
a professional organizer.

I clean and organize homes
of someone who's just
passed away
to make it easier on their loved ones . . .

But all I can say:
Mom, you clean the homes
of dead people?

UNIFORM

Mom's uniform
isn't a maid's uniform,
not what I was expecting.

It looks like she's in an astronaut costume,
like Nurse Donna.
She has a face mask,
outerwear,
and
FLATS.

WAYS TO SAVE MONEY

Mom mixes water
in our soap bottles
(shampoo too),
to make it
last.

Takes us to Kroger
not Publix
(where shopping is a pleasure),
where Ibrahim gets free cookies
and I get a bite
if I'm lucky.

Mom doesn't waste money on crackly packages
of cakes or cookies.
Mom now wears flats (to work),
punches in her Kroger Plus number,
eyes smile when the price numbers drop.

LUNCHES

If you were to compare lunches
when Abba was here—

When Abba was here,
he would pack us
crackly packages
with a smiling girl
Little Debbie
on them.
A comma of cream
rolled in perfect
chocolate
cylinders.

Now that Abba's gone,
Mom packs us splotchy red apples.
Spheres of nothing special.

MOM'S NEW JOB

Mom cleans our house less
(*organizes* she says),
other people's homes more.

Now when I walk,
my feet make friends
with crumbs.

DADA ABU

The bill (just one for now)
comes in the mail,
has 5 digits on it.
The numbers aren't shy,
they are
bold.

This bill Dada Abu tries to fold
into a teeny-tiny square
and take to his room.
But Mom stops him first.

Her words pour out,
Let me see it
Now.

A wrinkle pops up
lies down
between her eyebrows.

Amazing how a paper
so light
can
weigh
so much.

I know I don't have insurance
but I have savings.
I'm going to be paying.
I'm not a burden.
You've already done so much.

Usually Mom would argue
but this time
her lips stick out,
cheeks puff,
keeping all her words in.

MEETING WITH THE DOCTOR

This time
we go into a room
with extra-comfortable sofa chairs.

I thought this treatment was
supposed to work?

Well, there's a 20 percent chance it'll fail.

Why weren't we informed
about the percent of failure?

You never know with medicines.
There's always a risk.
Some treatments work.
Some don't.

Don't worry.
We'll move on
to the next treatment.

But I can see the way
Mom's lips button,
worry glossed all over them.

NEXT TREATMENT

Today Dada Abu
is in Chemo Infusion Room 1,
a room with an actual door,
the fanciest room on the ward,
while he gets different medicine
and extra attention.

Even though
he gets the fancy room
he looks right then left,
eyes t-w-i-n-k-l-e.
He leans forward
as far as he can,
which isn't that far
because he's plugged into an IV
that drip
              drip
                      drips.

Between you and me,
cancer sucks!

IRONY

Bad news goes with soft chairs
and free parking.
Good news goes with hard chairs
and you have to pay for parking.
I'd rather we paid for parking,
sat on a hard chair,
to get good news.

At the exit of the parking lot,
there is a man complaining
about paying for parking.
I wish we weren't in the chemo infusion center
that gives out free parking vouchers.

Paying for parking means
we wouldn't be here for
chemo.

THE
PLAN

PART NINE

❀

WRISTS

RAINY DAY

I've been spending more time on the courts,
less time in Zaina's room
to make sure I make good choices.
Not borrowing anything.

But today the clouds are sobbing,
thunder, lightning, and rain,
which means tennis practice is canceled,
which means I'm going to say yes
when Zaina texts
A to Z?

This time I stuff my bag
with its laughing mouth
into my closet.

COMPARISONS

Zaina has 3 sisters
each 3 years apart,
except Muzna
who's 4 years older
than Khadeejah.

Zaina = 13
Salma = 16
Khadeejah = 19
Muzna = 23

I wish Zaina was my sister
but the thing about Zaina's 3 sisters
(this is why I'm a teeny bit glad
I don't have any)
is that you're always being
compared to them.

We know Muzna is the prettiest,
but we know it most today
by the way her clothes

and eyelashes
flutter *look-at-me*.

Muzna models a lehenga.
Creamy white
with a froth of pink.

Muzna models a gharara.
Classic maroon
with pops of gold.

Muzna models a shalwar kameez.
Emerald green with dangling pearls.

For each outfit
Muzna matches her jewelry.

This one was Nani Ami's wedding set.
Look at how skinny
her wrists must have been.
She passed it to Nani,
then Mom,
then me.

Muzna says *me*
in a whisper,
like she still doesn't believe
she's getting married.

I want to inch closer,
study the poetry and patterns
of her jewelry.

But I don't want to touch it,
can't touch it,
fold my wrists
just to be safe . . .

WEIRD BUT TRUE FACT #11
Did you know that if you touch something,
you're more likely to purchase it?

SECRETS

Mom doesn't tell
her aunty friends
about Abba.

Even though
the aunties remind me of
a gentle flock of birds,
I think Mom sees them
as angry buzzing bees.

NAZAR

On the phone
Dadi's voice crackles
as she says
All this must be caused by nazar.
Before we had wealth,
before we had health.
Now we're struggling.

Nazar—
Urdu word for
the evil eye.

Dadi tells Mom
We had money,
a strong and complete family,
now we don't.

DADI'S OPINION

Before, when we were rich
and Dada Abu was healthy
and our family was together,
maybe we were *too happy.*

Maybe we flaunted it
and now we're floundering.

On the phone Dadi says,
Be careful what you share,
who you share joy with.
Not everyone
is happy for you . . .

ON THE WAY HOME
FROM SCHOOL

Howell Mill Road

Jeni's Ice Cream

(scoops and memories: $4.50 for two small scoops)

Anthropologie

RaceTrac

Used Tires

Pawnshop

      with a big sign

           WE BUY GOLD.

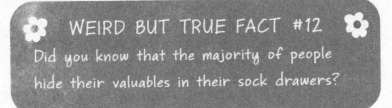

WEIRD BUT TRUE FACT #12
Did you know that the majority of people hide their valuables in their sock drawers?

WINDOW

I texted Zaina
      A to Z?
But she didn't answer
and looking outside
I see Zaina and her sisters
with their father.
A flick of her father's wrist
and a football goes high
a quick catch by Zaina.
Smiles.
Laughs.
Normally I'd run over
but today my feet
feel really really heavy.

WHAT I WANT

A happy family
(I need to do something about it).

SUNDAY SCHOOL

Actions are judged by intention.
If I'm just trying to help
then the way I help
should be
okay.

MUZNA'S GOLD

My intention
is to help Abba.
My intention
is to help Dada Abu.
My intention
is to help Mom.

 184

BEDTIME

Before
Abba would read Ibrahim
Chicka Chicka ABC.
He would make goofy sounds
and goofy hands
when all the alphabet letters fell
off the coconut tree.
Chicka chicka
BOOM BOOM!
But now Abba's gone
and when I try to read
to Ibrahim,
he asks for Abba.
Abba used to rub his back.
Big circles
then small circles.
When I try to rub Ibrahim's back,
my circles come out
medium
and Ibrahim
swats my hands away,
calls for Abba in a louder voice.

When he's all cried out,
I hug him.
I whisper
(Is it just air or a promise?)
I have a plan:
I'll bring him back, okay?

THINGS THAT KEEP ME UP AT NIGHT

1. **Muzna's Dholki**
A party to celebrate
her getting married
next Saturday.

2. **The Pawnshop's Words** *WE BUY GOLD*
Blinking on and off
in my memory.

3. **We Need Money**
God knows Zaina's family is fine.
Mine isn't.

SAYING OF DADA ABU:

A leopard doesn't change its spots.

It means people don't really
change.

I wish I could
Actually
Literally
Truly
Change.

GOLDEN GIRL PLAN

I flip pages
in my notebook,
looking for the perfect facts.

FOOD FOR THOUGHT

When Abba was here,
we would walk to the tennis courts.
Abba would carry
a palm full of salted pistachios,
sprinkling shells as he walked.

Now Abba's not here
and I don't believe in luck . . .

We don't have peanuts
but my fingers smile
as I reach for the pistachios.

ME

I'm really a good person,
I'm just
saving
all
my bad deeds
for this
one
thing . . .

PART TEN

BLADDER

MUZNA'S DHOLKI

I pray my maghrib,
ask for guidance,
dress in a peacock-blue silk shalwar kameez
with gold and red circles holding hands
that's sure to dazzle,
get the most compliments.

Even though Zaina and I
are too big to wear the exact same clothes anymore
we both plan to wear peacock blue.

My hands shake,
reach into the black of my closet,
search for the handbag
with the laughing mouth.

JEWELRY

Mom passes me a set of gold jhumka earrings.
Mom, why don't we sell our gold?

Mom sighs,
confides
We already sold some,
we're keeping these.
It's an investment.
The value of gold keeps going up.

Mom turns the earrings
over in her palms.
Right hand to left hand,
left hand to right hand.

My mom gave me these,
they used to be her grandmother's.

Then Mom's eyes get sharp.
Besides, we're doing just fine.

But Abba isn't here—
How are we going to . . .

We're fine, Aafiyah. Fine.
Let me zip you up.

But my outfit has buttons,
not a zipper.

DHOLKI

T-w-i-n-k-l-i-n-g lights
Flickering candles
Floating incense
Painted red lips

Girls in a ring
on fat mirrored cushions,
sing and clap.
As the dhol drums,
my heart matches its tune.

I say salam,
smile and thank aunties
when I get
compliment
upon compliment.

Elder aunties
cup my face
with their smooth
Oil of Olayed hands
searching for answers,
or beauty,
while I focus on
my bladder.

WHAT I DRINK

1 can of Coke
1 bottle of water
1 orange soda

My bladder is full.
I really

        really

                need to go.

BATHROOM

Now

    that my bladder's full,

Now

    I need to find a bathroom,

Now

    it's time to make a decision.

AM I GOING TO GO THROUGH WITH THIS???

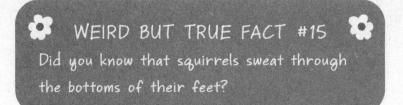

WEIRD BUT TRUE FACT #15
Did you know that squirrels sweat through the bottoms of their feet?

I feel like I'm sweating everywhere.

I'm just going to the bathroom,
right?

If her door's open
        I'll look.

If not,
        that's a sign.

I'll use the bathroom.
Go home.
Forget about this . . .

TEMPTATION

Her door
is open
a crack.

With a full bladder,
my decision comes
too easy.

I'll just take a *quick* peek . . .

In Muzna's room
I hold her card
like a shield.
I rehearse
I was just putting this here for you.

If I get caught—
I'm just leaving this here . . .

I feel my heart
thump thump thump,
the feeling in my stomach

punch punch punch,
feel the itch in my fingers
tingle tingle tingle.
Bladder pressing
as I reach for her dresser.

MUZNA'S DRESSER

Shirts
Pants
Blouses
Nothing.

How many clothes can one person have?

 200

UNDERWEAR DRAWER

Nothing.

SOCK DRAWER

Supposed to be where
most people hide their valuables.

MUZNA'S SOCK DRAWER

Just a lousy old journal.

HIJAB DRAWER

Last chance.
I stick my hand
underneath
nylon
chiffon
cotton
fluffiest silk.

4 velvet boxes.
Box on box on box on box.

Do I take them?
I think of Abba
       stuck without a passport.
I think of Abba
       going to jail again.
I know
       what I need to do.

I grab the boxes,
close the drawer,
put them in my bag.
RUN to the bathroom.

BATHROOM

Relief.
My fingers fumble with latches.
Box #1 is empty.
Is she wearing the jewelry?

So much for having a full bladder.
This was a BAD decision.

BOX #2

Gold blinks.
Winks back at me.
Rubies red as raspberries
that look good enough to eat.
I swallow my gasp.
I did it.

A new relief.
Followed by dread.
Followed by relief.

BOX #3

Emerald
upon gold
upon pearls.
Heavy and cold
in the palm of my hand.

BOX #4

Diamond set,
a stack of gold bangles.
Ten thin as hair
four thick as rope.

I stack the boxes.
Tell myself
I'm doing this
for my family.

I zip my bag.
The laughing mouth
changes into
a straight line.

My heart still drumming
with the dhol
all the way
back to the party.

DINNER

On a wilted paper plate
I nibble
biryani,
golden-orange-beige
grains,
nihari,
meat so tender it melts.

Normally I'd eat it all,
staining my fingers with
saffron and turmeric gold.

But even though I'm hungry
my mind is stained with
another type of gold.

My stomach is churning
round and round
like a washing machine.

I can't even taste the spices.

PART ELEVEN

MOUTH

HOME SAFE

I place the jewelry high on my dresser
in the first drawer
where no one ever looks.
My body stops feeling so shaky.
My mind gets nice and quiet again.

Tomorrow in the daytime
before my big tennis tournament,
I'm going to bike over to the pawnshop
the one that says *WE BUY GOLD.*
Then put the money
in the mailbox for Mom
(she won't know it's from me).
I'll fix the mess we're in
once and for all.

THE SETUP

Tomorrow's high
61 degrees Fahrenheit
the perfect day for biking
or a quick errand.

On my bike ride
to the pawnshop,
I'll need a bag
that's easy to wear.

I empty my book bag
of gum wrappers and notebooks,
clear my mind of doubt,
make space for 3 boxes of jewelry.

After tennis,
Mom will check the mail,
which is when I'll have
a blank
but hopefully full
envelope

sandwiched between bills
waiting for her in the mailbox.

Into the book bag
I slide my wallet
empty . . .
for now.

THE NEXT MORNING

I wake up,
remember the gold in my dresser.
Guilt feels yucky.

My insides feel like they're walking
downstairs with dread.

But then when I
think of Abba
think of Abba
think of Abba,
my insides feel like they're
floating with hope.

BATHROOM MIRROR

Before I bike over to the pawnshop
I peek at Muzna's jhumka earrings,
the ruby choker,
the small raspberry studs,
the gold bangles.
No time to try them on.
I'm on a mission.

After we pray
Mom reads aloud.
Oh Allah, give us aafiyah
Oh Allah, ease our problems
Oh Allah, help us bring Abba back

AFTER NAMAZ

Ibrahim walks over.
Naughty smile,
mouth stuffed
with mischief.

Ib,
do you have anything
in your mouth?

Open your mouth!

Ibrahim smiles
tight-lipped.
Mom sighs
as Ibrahim toddles away.
That kid needs to stop
putting things in his mouth.

Mom
Pins
Him
Down.

Scoops
out only air.

Ibrahim's face
reddens,
mouth trapezoidal.

Suddenly
his coughs are all weird.
Gagging sounds,
something's wrong
his eyes whine.

Mom's voice changes
into one I never want to hear again.

He's choking!
Grab my phone!
Call 911!

Mom's voice shriller,
Ibrahim's face redder.

Mom thumps his back
again and again.
His face changes
into coughs.
Mom scoops out something.
I think I got it.

My heart beats in my ears
my chest
my throat.

I run over,
Mom's phone in my hand.

Ibrahim's face pink,
not red anymore
but still crying.

Mom hugs Ibrahim
forehead to forehead.
She breathes in
heavy and loud.
He breathes out
heavier and louder.

Her fingers
lick the tears off his cheeks.
Her hand
pat pat pats
circles on his back.

Mom studies
the wet thing in her hand,
mouth open in shock.
A gold, raspberry-like ruby earring
looks at me.

The room
gets
very
very
very
Quiet.

AFTER

THE

PLAN

PART TWELVE

EYES

BUT HOW?

Quick peek into my room,
the chair is pulled up to my dresser.
Ibrahim
Ruined
Everything.

MOM'S VOICE

A dangerous whisper.
Shaky hands.

Whose is this?

SILENCE

This silence
is anything
but
golden.

2 QUESTIONS

Where did this come from?

Although I'm not wearing makeup
my face is bronzed in guilt.

MOM'S NEXT QUESTION

A wobbly whisper,
Did you steal this?

MY ANSWER

My words
are a prayer.
Please Please
Don't Tell Abba.

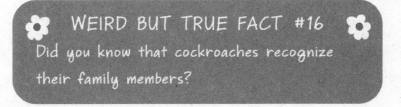

WEIRD BUT TRUE FACT #16
Did you know that cockroaches recognize
their family members?

If Abba was in this room
right now,
would he recognize me?

MOM'S FACE

Everything is
saggy
and
sad
looking.

Everything is
too still,
too sore,
too quiet.

Mom, I can explain . . .

MOM SCREAMS

If anger was a tune,
I've never heard those notes before.

When Mom's tune
becomes recognizable,
the questions begin.

Why did you do this?
Whose jewelry is it?
Why would you do such a thing?
Have you stolen before?

Me:
I wanted to
help Abba
come back,
sell Muzna's jewelry
and get the money
so you could pay
better lawyers.
So you could get
Abba back . . .
You could even pay
for Dada Abu's chemo . . .
I've seen the bills . . .

MOM

Aafiyah,
we have money for the lawyers.
Maybe not as much
as we usually do.
Things are harder.
We're   s t r e t c h i n g
but we can do this.

Dada Abu's bills
we can pay in installments,
a little at a time.

Abba's lawyers get paid a lot.
Too much.
But we're almost
at the end of this case.
We really almost are.
You didn't need to do
*something **like this**!*

You could have
Just

Talked
To
Me . . .

Mom brings her face
close to mine,
which makes me swallow harder.

PROBLEM

I don't know what I'm going to do . . .

MOM'S SOLUTION

We are walking right over.
You are fixing this.
Do you understand?

No more.

Don't ever STEAL again.
I DON'T CARE
      how much you miss Abba,
how poor we get,
we're fine
(her voice cracks here).

You never ever STEAL.
You're not Robin Hood!
We
(her voice cracks here too)
raised you to be better than that.

 228

I DON'T CARE if anyone saw you
or didn't see you.
God sees you.
Don't you care?

Mom's voice drains.
Mom's face changes too.
Her voice is now
even quieter
and scarier.
Aafiyah Qamar,
This is stealing.
You're a thief!

Hearing that word
makes me very cold inside.
Cold tears are the worst.

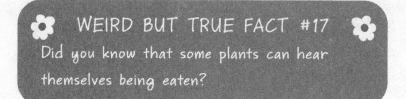

WEIRD BUT TRUE FACT #17
Did you know that some plants can hear
themselves being eaten?

I feel like one of those plants . . .

ANSWER

I'm crying too hard
to say *I do care.*

These tears are cold
they match the coldness
of my heart.
Ibrahim is watching,
still snuffling
and when I hug him
I wish I could absorb
his heart   his tears   his snot.
I feel so bad.

I don't know
whose tears are whose,
whose snot is whose.

🌸 WEIRD BUT TRUE FACT #18 🌸
Did you know that mice can feel each
other's pain?

Does Ibrahim feel my pain?
Does Mom?
Abba? Dadi?
Dada Abu?

HOW I FEEL

Intentionally left blank.

HOW MOM FEELS

You better start thinking
of what you're going to say,
how you're going to apologize.

Don't even get me started
on what people are going to say about you.

I'm taking a quick shower,
then we're leaving.

STAIRS

Before her foot is on the first step,
Mom's face looks splotchy.
She turns and walks
up the stairs,
leaving me alone
with my thoughts.

MOM'S SHOWER

Will probably not be quick,
will probably be slow,
because I have a hunch
she's going to cry
in the shower
first.

TIME

Mom will probably
need to fix her face
after crying,
conceal her red eyes.
A quick glance at the clock—
I have at least
30 minutes . . .
I dry my tears.
If Zaina, Muzna, Naheed Aunty know,
this will change everything.

234

The question that we joke about
Log kya kahenge?
What will people say?
is braided into my existence,
a joke no more.

ZAINA

If Zaina finds out
I'm a thief,
she won't want to be my friend.
I'm going to lose
the only friend
I ever had . . .

Having your best friend
live almost next door,
and not be your best friend
anymore?

I already lost Abba.
I can't lose Zaina.
Oh God,
I'm so sorry.

MESS

I got myself in it.
I can get myself out.

WEIRD BUT TRUE FACT #19
Did you know that every single ant in a
colony has a job?

This is my job.

6:33 P.M.

Golden hour:
The sun is gold,
slipping away.
I get on the prayer mat.
Pray
the prayer Mom taught me ages ago,
a melodious memory.

Oh God,
Separate me from my sins
Like you separate East and West

Oh God,
Cleanse me from sins
as white clothing is cleansed of dirt,
Wash away my sins
with water   with snow   with hail

More tears begin to flow.

25 MINUTES

I can fix this.
   I'll just pop over next door—
  Put it all back.
  Start over.
   You know?

22 MINUTES

I grab my bag.

19 MINUTES

Wipe off Ibrahim's spit,
polish the ruby gold earring
(that looked good enough to eat).
Press it back in the soft foam,
close the velvet box,
latch it tightly.
  Gotta go.

RUN NEXT DOOR

Without Mom
who's still in the shower.
I'll be real quick.

Zaina's mom, Naheed Aunty,
gives me a warm hug,
which makes my eyes squirm,
makes my face suck in
all the leftover tears.
I run upstairs to see Zaina.
Music is shimmying Zaina around.
Where's Muzna?
Zaina's eyes roll.
She went to get her nails done.

I'll be right back . . .

MUZNA'S ROOM

My fingers are tingling.
Heart beating in my ears so loudly.
I don't remember all the drawers

Undies
        Socks
                Hijabs

Fingers tremble
as I start to place the boxes
underneath the shimmery pile.

My heart is beating
in my ears fiercely
Zaina's music is loud,
and I do have mild hearing loss
so I don't hear the footsteps . . .

MILD HEARING LOSS

May be the reason

I don't hear
Muzna's feet—

MUZNA'S QUESTION

What are you doing in my room?

BUSTED

Muzna's jewelry boxes
poke their heads out
of the drawers,
sticking their tongues out
at me.

ANOTHER QUESTION

Why are you touching my jewelry?

Muzna's name
means cloud bearing
rain.

A storm cloud would be better
than this.

MY ANSWER

Nothing.
My mouth open.
No words come out.
My tongue is swollen with tension.
Can't answer even if I wanted to.

WHAT DOES HAPPEN

Even though
my brain must be cooling,
my face is turning hot
and my eyes sting
with tears.

I blink them away,
mind screaming
Don't cry
Don't cry
Don't cry.

Instead, I croak
It's not what it looks like . . .

Muzna's mouth
twists and snaps.
Why don't you explain?

My best friend
Zaina is in the room now,
and when she opens her mouth
she only says
Are YOU the one
who's been taking
my things?

My hands find my face.
I hide behind my hands.
What burns the most
is that Zaina doesn't even wait
for me to answer,
doesn't even wait
for me to explain . . .

Zaina who is
always laughing,
Zaina who is
always talking,

Zaina who is
always sharing,
doesn't waste
any words on me.

Just stares at me
shaking her head.
The irony isn't lost on me.

Muzna walks over
hands rough,
doesn't care that her hijabs
once in perfect squares
are now angry ovals,
yanks the boxes out of the drawers.

These belonged to my Nani Ami!
My sisters and I DON'T
want to see you here anymore . . .

FAREWELL

I think
even if I tried to explain,
it wouldn't work.

I, Aafiyah Qamar, am a thief.

ESCAPE

I run down the stairs
out the door
past the sidewalk
into my house,
safe once more.

5 MINUTES OVERTIME

At home
Mom's makeup didn't work
very well,
because her eyes are still red,
which means she cried a lot.

Aafiyah, are you ready?
Her outlined eyes narrow.
Heels click clack,
walks over to me by the door.
Where've you been?

All the words
that were stuck in me
now come out too fast.
I went next door to return the jewelry,
but Muzna saw me putting it back
and now everyone is going to think,
to know, that

I'm a thief.

FRONT DOOR

I sink down
put my head
between my knees,
like Nurse Donna said to do
when I feel woozy.
Except I don't feel woozy,
I just feel very very cold
and very very heavy.

❀ WEIRD BUT TRUE FACT #22 ❀
Did you know that a rain cloud weighs as
much as 100 elephants?

Even though there's no rain
the air feels heavy as 100 elephants
if not more.

AFTERMATH

Mom's angry face
wilts.

Oh, Aafiyah,
what you do
isn't who you are,
you just made some
really bad decisions.

Mom's feet
kick her heels off
in an X.

She leaves them
in a messy pile,
even though she always tells me
to move mine.

She puts one hand
on my back,
cups my face
in the other.

Before I know it

tears,

the cold ones

I'd been trying so hard

to keep in,

slip from my eyes.

WEIRD BUT TRUE FACT #23
Did you know that raindrops are shaped
like hamburger buns?

My tears

are shaped like

shame.

DADA ABU

Buttons his blazer,
I'm ready.

Mom and I are confused.

Your game?

My game?

Today is the big tournament,
us against Lakeside.
I'm supposed to be there
in 30 minutes.

The drive
to the game
is very very quiet.

ON THE COURT

I fumble with my racket,
keep hitting the ball into the net.
Coach Baker calls me over,
tells me to make sure
I follow through.

I lift the racket over my shoulder,
make sure the ball goes over the net—

but all I can think of
is how I wish I hadn't followed through
with my plan . . .

MIXED DOUBLES

I lose game after game
against my opponent.
I hit ball after ball
into the net.

After I lose horribly in singles,
Ciara wants to know
what's wrong.
Coach Baker wants to know
if I'm feeling okay.
Dada Abu's looking at me
with the words *I know* in his eyes.

I don't have time to talk to them
because I'm up next.
I'm supposed to play in mixed doubles
and the only relief I have is knowing that
Imran doesn't talk,
won't ask me any questions.

Imran slices the ball easily,
spins it too,

but even though I'm hitting the ball
over the net
a quarter of them are out.
My feet can't seem to run fast enough
to reach the ball,
to hit them back,
even though I'm trying.

Fact: I'm the reason we lose.

WHAT IMRAN SAYS

Nothing.

WHAT I SAY

I'm sorry.

I walk over to Dada Abu.
Let's go home.

AFTER THE MATCH

Mom walks over.
Her face no longer shaken,
now determined.

Coach Baker,
Aafiyah won't be playing
for the time being.
She's made some poor choices at home.
She needs to work on
some personal development.

Coach Baker asks:

256

When will she be back?
Mom turns a shoulder
(only one),
her hand grabbing my arm too hard.
It's indefinite . . .

ON THE WAY HOME

If I thought the drive to the courts was quiet,
the drive back home is even quieter.

Until Dada Abu says,
Aafiyah,
have you heard the hadith
"O Son of Adam,
Even if you have a valley full of gold,
you'd still want more"?

PART THIRTEEN

PALMS

JIGSAW

Mom picks me
up
piece by piece,
puts me back together
like a puzzle.

Tell me everything.

And I do.

MOM'S CONSEQUENCES

You're lucky.
You know the signs
of your stomach,
your fingers,
your heart.
When you feel like that,

just stop.
Walk away . . .

In the meantime,
no more tennis practice
no more going over to friends' houses.
(Zaina wouldn't invite me anyway.)
No more phone.
(Zaina's the only person who texts me.)
Until you can figure yourself out . . .

Think of the consequences.
Think of getting caught.
Think of the person you're hurting.
It's stealing.
Abba is hurt,
because someone else stole.

It's haram.
As Muslims, we strive to
follow and obey God.

    Mom, what am I going to do without tennis?
Mom smirks.

You should have thought of that
before you tried to pull off such nonsense.

You're going to help out around here.
Go with Dada Abu to the masjid.
Go with Dada Abu to chemo.
Take Ibrahim to the park.
Do some chores . . .

Mom holds out her hand,
I reach out mine to shake it.
Mom's mouth puffs out air,
lets out a real smile.
Your phone, silly goose!

Oops!
I place my phone in her open palm.

SUNDAY SCHOOL

On the Day of Judgment,
we will be handed our records.
Good records go to your
                right hand.
Bad records go to your
left hand,

and on the scale
they'll weigh all the good deeds
and if it's heavy enough,
if the record goes to your right hand,

you'll go to heaven
where there will be rivers of milk
and rivers of honey.

Sister Amani
waves her hands as she talks,
makes her hands flow like rivers.

All I can think about:
What if my bad outweighs the good?

What if my record
goes to my left hand?
Then what?

MOOD

Even though
it's springtime in Atlanta
(so many months of Abba being gone),
and usually I would enjoy
nodding daffodils,
branches weighed down with pink flowers,
golden sunshine,
nothing matters anymore.

I belong
in the sky above the moon,

where my mood
matches the sky.

LUNCHTIME

Usually I sit
with Zaina,
but this time
Zaina doesn't even look
my way,
not a peek.

I should have tried harder
to make more friends
but the problem with having
such a good friend
is that the others
don't really matter . . .

I wish it was illegal
in Atlanta
for one person to sit alone
at lunch.

THE NEXT DAY

I shove my half-eaten
cheese sandwich
into the trash,
head to the library,
browse my Weird but True! book
and wish that I wasn't so weird anymore.

CHORES

Mom makes me
peel purple papery onions
    dirty golden potatoes,
wash white scattery rice
and soak it too.

Mom makes me
watch and learn,
to see how she cooks
hard circles of brown dal
until they become
spicy, simmery,
and soft.

Mom makes me:
spray counters,
discard peels,
wash curried pots,
take out the trash,

studies my lips
to make sure
not one complaint
leaves them.
Not one.

LOW

Mom senses my moods
after school,
tells me that Abba used to say
When you watch an airplane soar,
remember that it started out
on the ground.

In order for you to soar,
sometimes you have to start out

low.

ABBA'S CASE

When is Abba coming back?
I ask Mom
over and over
over and over.

Mom usually says
I don't know . . .
I hope soon inshallah . . .
Keep praying . . .

But this time
the forehead wrinkles
between her eyebrows
loosen,
look less like slices of cake.

She plays Abba's voice mail
on her phone's speaker.

The lawyer says
we may get a new judge

who will hopefully read the files
and know that we're right . . .

Send my love to Ib and FooFoo . . .

In my notebook of facts,
I turn to a brand-new page
write down what we need
to plan a Welcome Back party
    posters for the airport (the glitterier the better)
    balloons
    flowers
for Abba and Dadi.
I'm remembering what hope feels like.

CHEMO

Dada Abu
studies his numbers of cancer cells
like he studies the
seeds
     roots
        leaves
of his tomato plant—

often.

Even though he studies his plants,
reads Quran,
thinks positive,
prays,
the cancer's
still there.

DADA ABU'S DAYS

A pillbox of
days of the week
that pop up and down—

S
M
T
W
T
F
S

containing small circles,
long ovals,
and unanswered prayers.

TEST RESULTS

When Dada Abu
is on hold,
he puts the phone on speaker,
and if there's a sound
I hate more than anything
in the whole wide world,
it's the music on the phone
the music that taunts us
while we   wait   wait   wait
to hear the test results—
Nothing's Changed.

DADA ABU'S TOMATO

Ibrahim notices it first.
Smaller than his thumbnail,
round
    green
       perfect balls.
Sign of life

on a tall green stalk.
What makes me wilt
is knowing that Dada Abu's tomatoes are thriving
and he's not.

THINGS TOMATOES NEED
TO RIPEN

The right temperature
The right soil
The right water
The right sunlight.

THINGS DADA ABU NEEDS
TO HEAL

I don't know.

DADA ABU'S WEIRD BUT TRUE FACT

Dada Abu plucks a few green tomatoes off:
We need to let this plant breathe.

Sometimes a plant
has too many green tomatoes.
It takes too much energy to turn them
red.

Some gardeners remove
the smallest tomatoes
on a too-tired plant
so that the other tomatoes
can get the chance
to ripen.

REFLECTIONS

Sort of like dropping all the bad habits
to make your good habits
shine?.

PARK

I miss the tennis courts,
the place where I felt in control,
where my hands were
the good kind of busy
and I could feel the energy
of the racket strings
hitting the fuzzy ball.

You would think that
going to the park is fun,
but going to the park
with Ibrahim
means all I do is

push him on the swings
back and forth

                   and higher
         and higher

until my arms hurt
and my hands too,
the bad kind of busy.

21 DAYS LATER

Dada Abu's tomato
turns red
but before we can pluck it,
Ibrahim grabs it
puts it in his mouth.

Dada Abu just laughs
At least he's putting something
in his mouth
that he can eat . . .

QUESTION TO GOD

How can tomatoes sprout
so freely
when cancer is taking over
Dada Abu?

BREAKTHROUGH

When Dada Abu asks Nurse Belinda
his numbers today,
we don't realize
we are holding our breath,
because as soon as she tells us
the cancer is reacting the way it should
the chemo is working the way it should
our breath turns into
laughter.

DADA ABU

Looks like we are going to
SMASH
that bowl pretty soon,
right?

CELEBRATE

That night
we go to Zyka.
Sit in the corner
with the least people,
the least germs.

Celebrate with spicy Chicken 65,
red as nail polish.
It makes my eyes tear.

Ibrahim rolls naan into fist balls,
scatters rice like confetti,
but our scolding voices are off today

as we melt over
mango ice cream—
clay pots of gold.

NEW HOBBY

Since Zaina's no longer friends with me
I spend a lot more time at home.
When Mom's not organizing
the homes of dead people,
she shows me
how to keep my hands busy.
How to loop plush yarn,
push a fat needle in,
pull it out,
link stitches together,
how to crochet something beautiful
from a plain ball of yarn.

COOKING

Over the stovetop
on medium heat
Mom adds

 1 cup flour
 ½ cup salt
 1 cup water
 1 tablespoon of oil
 2 teaspoons of cream of tartar
 Yellow food coloring

Mom won't tell me what she's making.
Just watch!

Mom stirs the mixture together
until it can't be stirred,
leaving a gloopy glaze on top,
evaporates all the water,

mixes everything into a golden ball.

Play dough!

Ibrahim and I
knead the ball
palm to palm,
roll it short
stretch it long
evaporate my sadness away.

MASJID

I don't just accompany Dada Abu
to chemo.
I also accompany Dada Abu
to the masjid.

Dada Abu wants to go to the masjid
for the five prayers
like he does in Pakistan—
Fajr at the thread of dawn
Zuhr when the sun is brave
Asr when the sun is shy
Maghrib when the sun is leaving
Isha when the moon is out.

But here in America
we don't have a driver
(just Mom).
Things are farther away,
so I go with him for just Isha.

At the masjid
I'm covered,
camouflaged.
You can see just my face and hands.

At the masjid
I'm learning what it's like
to be a moth,
muted,
and I like it.

Sometimes I want to be
the one
everyone looks at
and sometimes I
just want

to be invisible.

WHEN THE MOON GLOWS

Imran sometimes goes for Isha.
Sometimes he will nod at me
even though I'm not on the courts anymore.

Do you ever talk? I ask him.

I'm a man of few words.

A laugh tickles my throat,
escapes.

WEIRD BUT TRUE FACT #26
Did you know that you are 30 times more
likely to laugh with a friend than when
you're alone?

HISTORY

Zaina and I
have known each other
since we were babies.
Our moms tell us how
Zaina crawled first,
crawled circles around me
while I just sat there.
And then one day
I got up easily,
skipped over crawling
and started to walk,
toddled over to her.

Now Zaina and I
don't crawl to each other,
don't walk to each other,
don't talk to each other,
and I really need to fix it.

TENNIS

After many many days
of helping Ibrahim
helping Dada Abu
helping Mom,
Mom tells me
I've been a big help.
I'm not off the hook
but I can end
the tennis season
playing again.

My fingers can't wait
to twirl my racket,
throw the ball high,
blue sky up,
smack it down.
A perfect serve.

BFF NOTE

Best friends are supposed to
show each other
their happy sides
and their sad sides,
their good sides
and their bad sides.
Before I only showed Zaina
all the happy parts of me.

If I was a lake
I've only shown Zaina
my surface,
where golden sunlight reaches.

In my note to Zaina,
I tell her about all the deep
the dark parts of me
where golden sunlight doesn't touch.

I tell her about
what I stole,
why I stole,

what I plan to do
now.

In my note,
I drop all my worries in
like pebbles in a lake.

I tell her about Abba,
about Dada Abu,
about how not having her as a friend
makes me feel like
I'm a lake gone dry.

Under PS,
I invite her to my final match—
Saturday
3:00 p.m.
The Courts.
Will you please come?

I fold the note
the way Zaina showed me
when we didn't have phones to text

A to Z time?
Tucking my inky sorry
into neat triangles.

Heart beats,
stomach punches,
fingers tingle
(in a good way)
when I push the note into
the skinny mouth of her locker.

ABBA'S CASE

Keeps getting delayed,
moved from day to day
now month to month.

Seasons change.
Friends leave.

But now there's a new judge
and new hope.

ZAINA'S RESPONSE

Zaina doesn't reply to the note,
doesn't look my way.
I eat my soggy liquid gold
Velveeta mac and cheese
                        alone
again.

THE COURTS

I feel wobbly
at lunchtime at school.
I feel fidgety at home.
But back on the courts,
at tennis practice
before the final match,
I feel just right.

Coach Baker says *Welcome*,
Imran nods my way,
Ciara waves a smile,

Connor looks away and back again.

On the courts
my legs stand strong.

On the courts
the sound of the ball snapping
makes my feet bounce to its rhythm.

On the courts—
THWACK!
the sound of my racket
hitting the ball,
deep and far
over the net
inside the lines
helps me *THWACK!*
all my problems away.

MIXED DOUBLES

Connor and Ciara
high-five,
hug at a point,
smile at each other
when they say
the points out loud.
Especially when they get to say:
Love
Fifteen love
Thirty love
Forty LOVE
Game.

Imran knows the Muslim rules—
boys and girls
don't touch;
instead we
high-five rackets.

I like playing with Imran
because I get to focus on the game
and just the game.

THE FINAL MATCH

Run a lap to warm up,
shake out my legs,
stretch up to the sky,
lean down to the silver
loopy laces of my shoes.

My fingers tingle
(in a good way)
as I warm up,
flexing them back
and forth.

ALONE

Dada Abu sits very straight.
Mom sits and stands,
sits and stands
to chase after Ibrahim.

And I hate how
my eyeballs betray me
by looking around for Zaina.

SINGLES MATCH

I serve just right,
hit the ball with enough strength,
follow through with my strokes . . .

It's still not good enough.
I needed more.

BLEACHERS

On the bleachers
I look up up up
and this time Zaina
waves down at me.
And in one second
I feel good enough.

QUESTION

I don't have time
to say *salam*,
to see Zaina properly,
to ask about my note,
because Coach Baker calls me over
for the mixed doubles final.

One question keeps buzzing
in my mind.
Does this mean
that Zaina and I
are friends again?

MIXED DOUBLES FINAL

Imran will say one word here,
tilt his head there,
when the ball is right on the line.
Let a smile get close to his lips,
nod his head when we win,
the smile even closer to his lips
will then let two words escape:
Nicely Played.

MIXED DOUBLES

Imran and Aafiyah

Y'all look so cute together
drawls Ciara.

The happiness I felt
over winning
is like my sweat—
evaporated.

Don't they know
two brown people
don't always need
to be paired
together?

REACTION

My two eyebrows
become one.

I tell Ciara
Knock it off
but Imran
shakes it off
literally,
shrugs.
We won!
then gives me
a racket high five.

REALIZATION

It's a funny thing
about getting to know people.
The ones you thought
seemed so much like a
moth
suddenly seem like a
butterfly.

WHAT I GET

From Mom:
a hug
from Dada Abu:
a pat on the back
from Ibrahim:
a sticky high five
from Zaina:
I don't know yet.

SURPRISE

Zaina and I
aren't huggers,
but this time
we hug.

It's as if no time
has passed.
Zaina leans in,
points to Connor,

whispers
That boy is cute.

I shake my head
and smile.
There's a lot
I haven't told you . . .

BACK TO NORMAL . . . ALMOST

Zaina's body curves easily
and when we walk and talk
her smile curves
just as easy.

But right now
her smile becomes a line.
What about
all those things
you
took?

My fingers squeeze
my tennis ball
hard.

The things you . . .
she looks down
stole?

She looks back up.
How do I know
you won't
do it
again?

I know all the right words
to tell Zaina
to reassure her
but right now
I don't know
what I can say
to tell her
that things
will be different.
I hold out my palms

empty
sweaty
but okay.

Instead
I'm going to show you,
prove it to you.
I don't want to be that person.
I'm not that person
anymore.

NIGHT

Today Zaina comes over to my house,
secrets spill out in seconds.

When Zaina invites me
back over to her house,
Mom says *not yet*

but soon

Inshallah . . .

NEW GIRL

I'm not that girl anymore,
the one who gives in to her whims,
that girl who borrows things from her
best friend
without asking.

This time,
I invite Zaina over
to my house.
I make Zaina's pineapple lip gloss
stand tall on my desk
ready to return.

Next time,
when I go to Zaina's house,
I roll my bag
place it in the trash can
push my palms
D
O
W
N
underneath onion peels
that wink back at me.

I don't wear my jeans with pockets.
Instead I choose leggings.

NEW JUDGE

This time
the new judge
listens to Abba's lawyer,
carefully reviews Abba's files,
the ones that tell the truth.
He says:
Innocent.
Case Dismissed.

BEST SELFIE EVER

Abba sends a picture
holding his passport,
looking almost the same.
His smile stretches
across his face,
his beard once pepper
now salt and sugar.

ANTICIPATION

At the airport terminal
we hold a *WELCOME BACK* poster
our fingers stained in glitter
and hope.

Everyone who comes out
that isn't Abba or Dadi
is wrong
and I feel my excitement

      s

          i

              n

                 k

into anger.

Where are they?

WHEN IT'S TIME

From a distance,
I see a head
I see shoulders
that look like Abba's.
The man stands just like Abba
and I know it's him.

Even though I'm not a YELLER,
When I say his name,
everyone around me turns,
even Abba from f   a   r away.

In my tennis shoes,
My feet are jumping jumping jumping.
Dadi waves her arms into a big V.
Abba's smiles are
slow and sure
and warm
like sunlight.

Bliss.

AIRPORT

I stop jumping
hold my camera lens still
and
wait   wait   wait.
If I zoom in,
now I can really see
Abba.

Ibrahim's curls float
when Mom holds him
over the railing
to Abba.

Dada Abu's glasses wobble
with joy when he sees Dadi.
I let my camera
click breathe click
in the moment
of a happy family.

The light is golden.

AUTHOR'S NOTE

In the Pakistani culture, gold is highly valued, and our jewelry is passed on from generation to generation. For example, the ornate jewelry set I wore at my wedding was passed on to my mother from my grandmother. Our jewelry is full of stories, memories, and love.

Although this story is fictional, I strung together experiences from my life. Like Aafiyah, I have mild hearing loss and cannot hear certain frequencies from my right ear, like crickets.

My father worked with airplanes in Abu Dhabi, the United Arab Emirates, and when I was a child, we used to only travel first class. I didn't know that it was a luxury at the time. When he changed his job, we traveled economy. I remember being surprised how different the experience was and missed first class!

As a teen, I had a friend who stole things from my

room. I remember her big tote bag and how swiftly things started to silently go missing. I should have confronted her but instead, I chose to avoid her. Initially, when I wrote Aafiyah's story, I had her not get caught when she put the jewelry back in Muzna's room. It was hard to write, but I changed the story because I realized I wanted Aafiyah to own up about her stealing, to learn how to have a difficult conversation, and to learn how to repair friendships.

Just like Aafiyah's family, there are innocent families who have gone through these similar experiences of detainment. My hope and prayers for these families are justice and reunification.

Like Aafiyah, I was on the tennis team in school and enjoyed playing with my father. Although my father and I share a love for tennis, not American football, when he would ask for us to throw him a roll of toilet paper, he would gleefully yell TOUCHDOWN! before spiking the toilet paper to the ground.

I love my grandparents and enjoy weaving them into my stories. I had cancer some years back and remember Nurse Donna fondly and how reassuring nurses can be. I also remember how isolating it was to be using a different bowl from the family and how horrendous that

ABC juice that my mother made tasted. I also remember my toddler falling sick a few days after I had my first chemo treatment. Typical!

Like Aafiyah, my eldest daughter loved National Geographic's Weird but True! facts. As research, I was asking aunties where they hid their gold when my nine-year-old daughter said that most people hid their valuables in their sock drawers and that she had learned this fact from her Weird but True! facts book. I read as many Weird but True! facts as I could, and Aafiyah's story started to blossom. My youngest daughter was like Ibrahim and loved to stand on the table, in the dishwasher, and also put small toys in her mouth. Life with a toddler had its frustrating moments, as does life with a family member who is undergoing cancer, but throughout all the moments that Aafiyah and I experienced, I strove to weave them with pieces of joy.

RESOURCES

Kleptomania is a disorder in which you are unable to resist the urge to steal items that you don't really need. If you don't treat the disorder, it can not only hurt you, but also your loved ones. If you feel this urge, please get help by telling an adult. Try to see a professional for a treatment plan. You may feel nervous or embarrassed, but without help, it may be challenging to overcome kleptomania on your own. Here are three tips that may help:

1.   **Recognize your triggers.** Certain situations or feelings may trigger your urge to steal.

2.   **Explore healthy outlets. Practice healthy** activities to rechannel your urge to steal. Exercise, like yoga, playing a sport, or other recreational activities like art or making a puzzle, can help you relax and manage your stress.

3. **Set goals and stay motivated.** Recovery from a disorder like kleptomania can take time. Stay focused by remembering your recovery goals. Think of your future self: by sticking to your goals, you can ensure a healthier and safer future for you. You can also strive to mend and maintain strong family and friend relationships during this time and throughout your life.

Helpful Links:

www.newportacademy.com/resources/substance -abuse/teens-and-kleptomania

www.mayoclinic.org/diseases-conditions /kleptomania/diagnosis-treatment/drc-20364753

GLOSSARY

aafiyah: Arabic word for *well-being*

aloo gosht: meat curry with potatoes. Aloo means *potato*. Gosht means *meat*.

Abba: Urdu (Pakistani language) word for *father*

Allah: Arabic name for God

biryani: spicy meat and rice cooked separately before being layered and cooked together.

chai: Urdu word for *tea*

Dada Abu: means *paternal grandfather* and is what Aafiyah calls her grandfather

Dadi: father's mother

dal: lentils

dhol: traditional drum and where the dholki ceremony's name originates

dholki: a ceremony or wedding party for women where they celebrate, sing, dance, and beat drums

gharara: a fancy outfit made with wide-legged pants that flare out at the knee. This is usually worn with a flowy kurta top and a dupatta (scarf). It is usually heavily embroidered.

gulab jamun: fried milk-based ball-shaped dessert popular in Pakistan. It is soaked in syrup infused with spices, such as saffron, cardamom, and rose water.

hadith: a record of the sayings of Prophet Muhammad.

haram: Arabic word that means *forbidden* and refers to actions that are not allowed in Islam

hijab: headscarf Muslim women or girls may wear

inshallah: God willing

jhumka: traditional bell-shaped ornate dangling earrings worn in Pakistan and South Asia

khair: Arabic word for *goodness*

khala: maternal aunt or mother's sister

lehenga: a fancy outfit usually made with a silky flowy skirt and a shorter top. It usually has heavy embroidery and an ornate dupatta.

mamu: maternal uncle or mother's brother

masjid: mosque or Muslim place of worship

naan: a type of flat bread

namaz: Urdu word for *prayer*. The Muslim prayer occurs five times a day. The five prayers are:

    Fajr: prayer between dawn and sunrise

    Zuhr: prayer after the sun has passed its peak

    Asr: prayer when afternoon shadows lengthen

    Maghrib: prayer just after sunset

    Isha: prayer around nightfall

Nani Ami: means grandmother's mother and is a name for a maternal great-grandmother

nazar: Urdu word that means *looking at*, but in this case the evil eye

nihari: a spicy tender meat stew eaten in Pakistan

paratha: delicious flatbread consisting of layers of cooked dough

qamar: Arabic word for *moon*. This is also Aafiyah's last name.

Salam: Arabic word for *peace*. Sometimes this is said as an abbreviation for Assalamualaikum, the Muslim greeting for "peace be upon you."

samosa: a triangular pastry that is either fried or baked and filled with spiced potatoes, onions, peas, cheese, meat, or lentils

shalwar kameez: a traditional dress worn by women and men in Pakistan. The top, or kameez, is loose. The pants are usually wide on the legs but cuffed at the bottom.

AAFIYAH'S ALOO GOSHT RECIPE

INGREDIENTS:

- 1 pound goat mutton, cut into small pieces
- 1 diced onion
- ½ teaspoon garlic paste
- ½ teaspoon ginger paste
- 1 teaspoon ground cumin
- 1 teaspoon ground coriander
- 1 teaspoon salt
- ¼ teaspoon turmeric
- ½ to 1 teaspoon red chili powder
- 1 15-ounce can tomato sauce
- 2 medium-sized potatoes, cut into cubes

Rinse goat mutton. Put it in three tablespoons of heated vegetable oil with the diced onion. Add the garlic, ginger, and spices and fry until the meat is lightly browned and the onions are golden.

Add the tomato sauce. Cover the pot on medium heat and cook until the meat is tender. The meat may take up to 2 hours to become tender. Once the meat is tender,* add chopped potatoes and cook in the sauce for 20 minutes until they are tender. Serve with rice or naan.

*If you use a pressure cooker, it can take 30 minutes to cook the goat mutton. Please make sure to have adult supervision.

ACKNOWLEDGMENTS

A BIG thank-you to:

My enthusiastic editor, Alyson Day, for your gorgeous, uplifting emails and for your passion for my stories. I love how you understand my characters and believe in them and me. Thank you for connecting with Aafiyah when she was just a tiny idea and a few lines of a story pitch and for falling in love with her from the beginning. I can't wait for more book adventures with you.

My dedicated agent, Rena Rossner, for your endless encouragement, being an editorial expert, and for knowing what my story and I need at all times. I'm so happy to be on this publishing journey with you. The best advice you gave me was to get started on book #2 ASAP and I'm so glad I listened and was able to get the bulk of this out before the pandemic started!

Anoosha Syed for bringing Aafiyah to life and to Molly Fehr for nailing yet another gorgeous cover!

HarperCollins team: Molly Fehr, Emma Meyer, Mitchell Thorpe, Shona McCarthy, Meghan Pettit, and Eva Lynch-Comer.

My SCBWI critique partners who read my story and offered encouragement, tweaks, and critiques: Melissa Miles, Keith Resseau, Amber McBride, Amy Board, Vicki Wilson, and Becky Sayler. And my first family readers: Sana Dossul and Huma Faruqi. Thank you for always seeing my story and guiding me on how to make it better.

Angela Krans and Jill Cobb, who let me bring my first few pages of this middle grade story to our picture book critique group at Howell Mill Starbucks and reassured me that I was on the right track and gave me ideas!

My eleventh-grade English teacher, Mrs. Patricia Dobbs Carman, for inspiring me to write.

All my writing friends and authors who help me boost my voice, including Dr. Salma Stoman, Sarah Stoman, Aya Khalil, Saadia Faruqi, Maleeha Siddiqui, Marzieh Abbas, and Rena's Renegades.

Ms. Asiya Little for being a vibrant teacher and for introducing Zineera to Weird But True! facts.

Zineera Malik for being a Weird But True! fact expert who set the tone for this book!

My entire family in Peachtree City, in Pakistan, and beyond.

Mom and Abajan (Nazia and Dr. Firasat Malik) for your endless support, love, and duas and for always being there for the children.

Dr. Amena Dossul and Asna Dossul—wherever you go, there is laughter. Thanks, Mustafa Zakaria, for that phrase!

My brothers, Hamzah, Talha, and Osman Faruqi. Thank you for always being there; I pray that we are always united.

My Peachtree City sisters—Maha Hosain, Luz Faruqi, Huda Ahmed, Mariam Shakeel—and cousin Ebrahim Zakaria.

Amma and Abba (Huma and Zaheer Faruqi) for aloo gosht salan and for showing me how to live life with patience even when there are trials. Thank you for your constant generosity, 501 dinners, and for watching the children whenever I go on book adventures.

Love and duas × infinity for my grandmothers, Nana (Zarina Zakaria) and Daado (Ismat Malik), who make the everyday moments magical.

My daughters, Zineera and Anisa, for watching Hanifa, baking us cookies, and for doing the chores while I wrote. Hanifa, for walking with me at all times. Thank you all for bringing me joy.

My husband, Naoman Malik, for your constant

support and for giving the girls Baba Time while I wrote. I look forward to all our adventures, including the last-minute ones.

From my first middle grade book, *Unsettled*, I've learned how *much* impact a librarian and teacher can make. Thank you for championing my stories and getting them into classrooms and into the hands of your students. It means the world! A special shout-out to *all* the incredible librarians/educators/authors, including #MGBookChat, #BookPosse, #BookExcursion, #BookAllies, #BookSojourn, #LitReviewCrew, Mrs. Ghazala Nizami, Dr. Gayatri Sethi, and Mr. John Schu.

Readers, thank you for picking up this book and for reading with me so far. I do so appreciate you and your kind reviews. I hope you'll stay with me for more.